A special gift

for

....

"'All you need is love.
But a little chocolate now and then doesn't hurt."

Schulz

PUFFIN BOOKS

UK | USA | Canada | Ireland | Australia
India | New Zealand | South Africa

Puffin Books is part of the Penguin Random House group of companies
whose addresses can be found at global.penguinrandomhouse.com.

puffinbooks.com

First published 2015
001

Copyright © Peanuts Worldwide LLC, 2015
peanuts.com

Peanuts created by Charles M. Schulz
Text by Lauren Holowaty
Line illustrations by Tom Brannon

The moral right of the author and illustrator has been asserted

Made and printed in China

A CIP catalogue record for this book is available from the British Library

ISBN: 978–0–723–29938–7

Happy Birthday Snoopy!

By **Charles M. Schulz**

PUFFIN

Meet the **Peanuts Gang**

PIGPEN

MARCIE

SALLY

has a crush on

likes to dance with

is best friends with

has a crush on

is the older brother of

CHARLIE BROWN

FRANKLIN

attends the same class as

PEPPERMINT PATTY

has a crush on

has a crush on

THE LITTLE RED-HAIRED GIRL

has a crush on

Charlie Brown was excited. His birthday was only a few days away and he couldn't wait.

"Do you know the BEST thing about birthdays, Charlie Brown?" asked Linus.

"Er, cake? Or presents?" replied Charlie Brown.

"No – **BIRTHDAY SURPRISES!**" said Linus.
"Everyone should get a surprise for their birthday!"

"Everyone?" asked Charlie Brown, looking confused.

BONK!!

"Maybe it doesn't matter **when** you surprise Snoopy," said Linus. "If he doesn't know when his birthday is, you could just walk up to him today and sing, 'Happy Birthday!'"

I COULD?

SURE.

So Charlie Brown marched straight up to Snoopy, who was taking a nap on his doghouse. He took a **deep breath . . .**

HA . . .

But a fly got caught in his throat
and all he could manage was . . .

NO WONDER I NEVER
GET ANY **SLEEP!**

COUGH!

SPLUTTER!

RATS!

Charlie Brown needed to
think of a **better** surprise.

Charlie Brown went to ask Lucy for her advice.

Lucy thought for a moment. "You need to sneak up on him with something really, really loud. **THAT** would surprise him!"

"But what if I surprise him **too much?**" asked Charlie Brown, a little unsure.

PSYCHIATRIC HELP 5¢

I'D TELL YOU BUT YOU'VE ALREADY USED UP YOUR **FIVE CENTS!**

THE DOCTOR

Charlie Brown told Sally all about how his
birthday surprises for Snoopy had gone wrong.

"Why don't you give Snoopy some
balloons?" said Sally. "Everyone loves
balloons. Balloons are the **BEST!**"

Charlie Brown and Sally set to work blowing up LOTS of balloons. They kept going until they were all **huffed** and **puffed** out.

WHAT COULD **POSSIBLY** GO WRONG WITH A BALLOON SURPRISE?

"It seems **A LOT** can go wrong with a balloon surprise, Charlie Brown," said Sally.

GOOD GRIEF, WHAT A DREAM! I'M GOING TO HAVE TO STOP EATING JUST BEFORE GOING TO BED!

HERE'S THE WORLD WAR I **FLYING ACE** COMING IN TO LAND! (WITH A LITTLE HELP FROM FRIENDS).

Poor Charlie Brown was more worried than ever.
This birthday surprise was so **terrible** he wasn't
sure he would EVER see Snoopy again.

Charlie Brown decided he would try one **last** birthday surprise for Snoopy. He would make him an AMAZING cake!

So that's **just** what he did.

(He also made an AMAZING mess, but the cake looked great!)

Charlie Brown headed outside
with his birthday surprise.

But Snoopy wasn't on his doghouse...

Charlie Brown searched **everywhere** for Snoopy.

He looked **high** . . .

He looked **low** . . .

He looked this way and that . . .

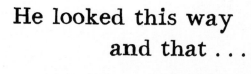

But Snoopy was **nowhere** to be seen.

The amazing birthday cake was not looking
quite so amazing any more, and
Charlie Brown was getting tired.

He gave up looking for Snoopy and headed home.

Charlie Brown had never been so surprised!

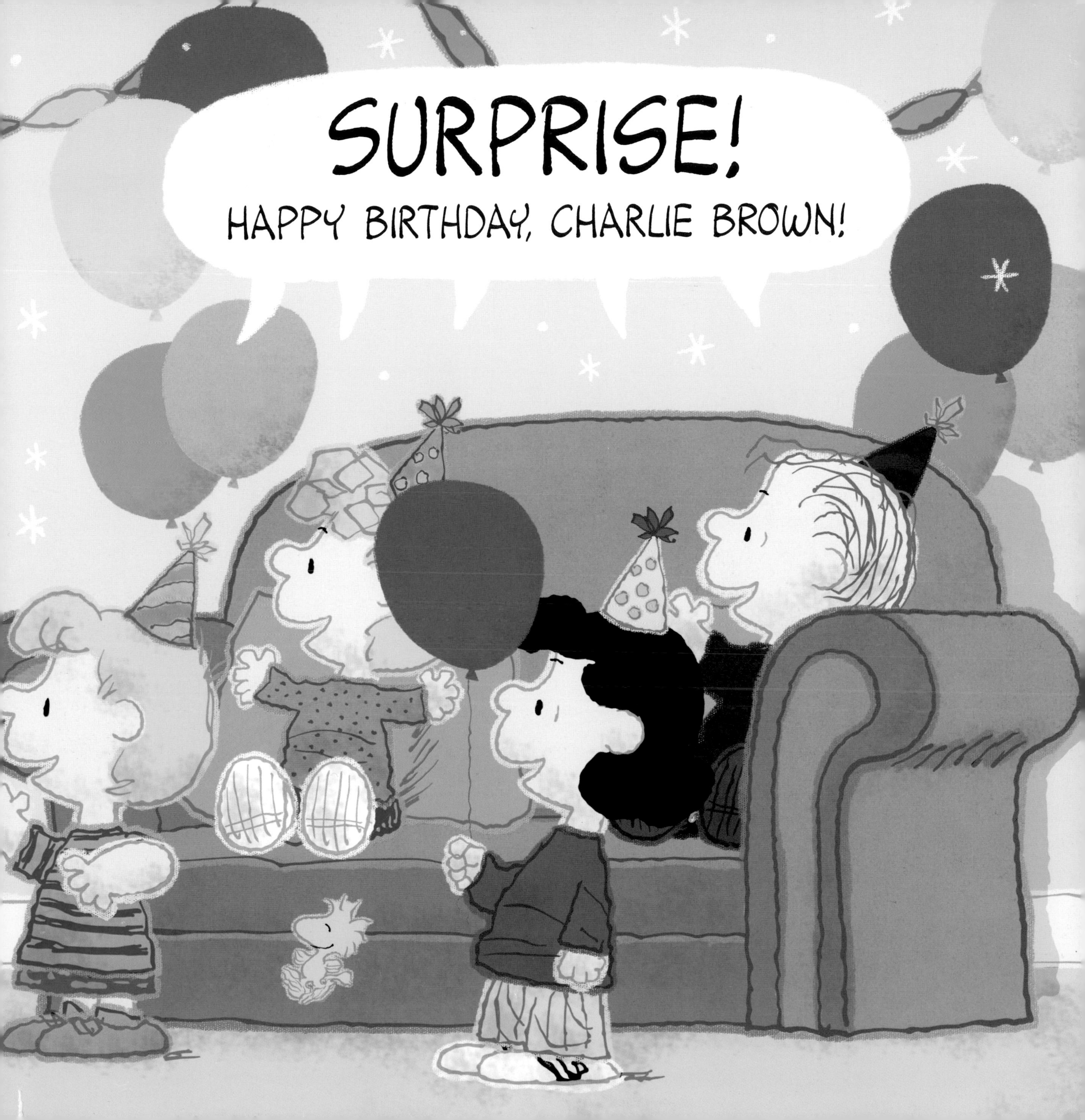
SURPRISE!
HAPPY BIRTHDAY, CHARLIE BROWN!

"Birthdays do have a habit of
snaking up and surprising
you!" said Peppermint Patty,
covered in melted icing
and licking her lips.

Charlie Brown had been **so busy** trying
to surprise Snoopy that he'd completely
forgotten about his **own** birthday!
Now he and Snoopy could
celebrate together.

*"Birthday surprises are the
best, aren't they, Snoopy?"*
said Charlie Brown.

IF YOU SAY
SO . . .

Birthday surprises are all very well, thought Snoopy, but **nothing** beats a nice peaceful **sleep.**

To Snoopy
Love Woodstock
XX

*HAPPY BIRTHDAY, SNOOPY!